LITTLE RUNNER

OF THE LONGHOUSE

LITTLE RUNNER

OF THE LONGHOUSE

LITTLE

RUNNER
OF THE LONGHOUSE

by BETTY BAKER
pictures by Arnold Lobel

HarperTrophy
A Division of HarperCollinsPublishers

Library of Congress Catalog Card Number: 62-8040
ISBN 0-06-020341-2 (lib. bdg.)
ISBN 0-06-444122-9 (pbk.)

First Harper Trophy edition, 1989.

for MEG

It was cold in the longhouse.

Little Runner jumped out of bed
and ran to the fire.

He sat down

with his father

and Little Brother.

His mother gave them

something to eat.

Many other Indians

lived in the longhouse, too.

There was always a lot to do,

but everyone helped.

17

Little Runner helped, too.

And he knew there

was a special time

to do each thing.

There was a time

to make maple sugar.

And a time

to put away the corn.

There was a time

to go hunting.

And a time to trade
with other Indians.

But Little Runner thought

the best time was today.

This was the time

of the New Year.

Today there would be dances

and games to play

and a lot to eat.

Soon men came

to dance in the longhouse.

When the dances were over,

other men came

to tell stories.

Everyone sat by the fire

to hear them.

Then some big boys
came to the longhouse.
The boys wore old clothes
and funny masks.

An old woman was with them.

She had a big basket.

It was the biggest basket

Little Runner had ever seen.

The big boys

went to each family

in the longhouse.

Each family gave them something

to put in the big basket.

29

30

Mother gave the boys

some maple sugar.

They put the maple sugar

in the basket.

Then the boys did a dance

to say thank you.

"Mother," said Little Runner.

"Why did you give the boys

the maple sugar?"

Mother said,

"If I did not give them

something for the basket,

they would take something.

Maybe they would take

my new moccasins.

Or my cooking pot.

Then I would have to buy it back.

I would have to pay for it

with *much* maple sugar."

"Oh," said Little Runner.

"That is fun.

I want to go with the big boys."

"Not this New Year," said Mother.

"When you are a big boy

you can go

with the basket woman."

Little Runner thought about it.

Then he put on a mask

and ran to his mother.

"Ha!" he said.

"I am a big boy.

And I want maple sugar.

Much maple sugar.

Give me maple sugar

or I will take something."

"Oh, big boy," Mother said.

"What will you take?"

Little Runner said,

"I will take the new moccasins
and the cooking pot."

"But I will see you,"
Mother said.

"And if I see you take them,
you must put them back.

That is the way it is."

"Oh," said Little Runner.

He took off the mask.

Little Brother said,

"Come play in the snow,

Little Runner."

Little Runner took Little Brother

to play in the snow.

They played snow snake.

Little Brother

was not very good.

He was too little.

But Little Runner

could make his snake stick

go far in the snow.

Then Little Runner saw the big boys

going from longhouse to longhouse.

He thought about the boys

and the maple sugar.

He looked at Little Brother.

Then he laughed.

Little Runner went
into the longhouse
and put on his mask.
"I am a big boy," he said.
"And I have Little Brother.
You would not give me
much maple sugar.
So I took Little Brother.
Now you must buy him back."
"Ah," said Mother.
"What do you want
for Little Brother?"

43

"A canoe," said Little Runner.

"What will you do

with a canoe?" said Mother.

Little Runner said,

"I will take the canoe

down the river

to get shells

to make wampum

to trade for all the maple sugar

I can eat."

"No," Mother said.

"A canoe is too much.

You can keep Little Brother."

Little Runner looked about.

Then he said,

"Will you give me

the three deerskins

for Little Brother?"

"What will you do

with three deerskins?"

Mother asked.

Little Runner said,

"I will trade the three deerskins

for a canoe

to go down the river

to get shells

to make wampum

to trade for all the maple sugar

I can eat."

"No," Mother said.

"Three deerskins are too much.

You keep Little Brother."

Little Runner thought.

Then he said,

"Will you give me

the big bow and arrows

for Little Brother?"

"What will you do

with the big bow and arrows?"

Mother asked.

49

Little Runner said,

"I will take the big bow and arrows

and hunt for three deer

to make deerskins

to trade for a canoe

to go down the river

to get shells

to make wampum

to trade for all the maple sugar

I can eat."

"No," Mother said.

"The big bow and arrows

are too much.

You keep Little Brother."

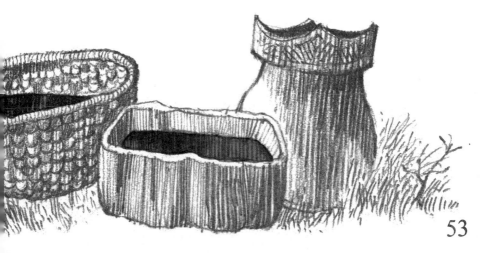

Little Runner thought some more.

Then he said,

"Will you give me a good knife

for Little Brother?"

"What will you do

with a good knife?"

asked Mother.

Little Runner said,

"I will take the good knife

and make a big bow and arrows

to hunt three deer

to make deerskins

to trade for a canoe

to go down the river

to get shells

to make wampum

to trade for all the maple sugar

I can eat."

"No," Mother said.

"A good knife is too much.

But I will give you

a big bowl of maple sugar."

"I will take it,"

said Little Runner.

"Now you can have Little Brother."

Mother laughed and said,

"But I HAVE Little Brother.

He came into the longhouse

with you.

He is sitting by the fire."

Little Runner laughed, too.

Then he took off his mask

and sat by the fire

with Little Brother.

Mother gave them a big bowl.

It was full of maple sugar.

All the maple sugar

Little Runner and his brother

could eat.